by Ernest Small

баба уага

illustrated by Blair Lent

HOUGHTON MIFFLIN COMPANY, BOSTON

for Theo

Acknowledgments

Baba Yaga is a traditional figure in Russian folktales who appears in many a story for Russian children. In this
book the author has drawn together into one story much of the Baba Yaga lore taken from such sources as:
Russian Wonder Tales by Post Wheeler, The Century Company, 1912 (new edition, Thomas Yoseloff, London,
1957); *Old Peter's Russian Tales* by Arthur Ransome, Thomas Nelson and Sons, Ltd., London, 1916 (reprinted
1960); *The Russian Grandmother's Wonder Tales* by Mrs. Louise (Seymour) Houghton, Scribner, 1906;
Siberian and Other Folktales by Charles Fillingham Coxwell, C. W. Daniel Company, London, 1925.

Deep in the darkest part of the forest, frail blackberry bushes and pale violets grew in patches of sunlight, but Marusia could not find what she was looking for.

The little girl's mother had sent her to the village to buy turnips, but Marusia had lost the money on her way. She had wandered into the forest to search for turnips that might grow wild.

Suddenly the ground began to tremble. Rabbits scurried under bushes and birds flew to the sky to hide in the clouds. Marusia put her ear to the ground. She heard a fearful thumping sound.

Marusia remembered what her mother had said: "Never enter the forest on the far side of the village, for that is the forest of Baba Yaga!"

"Whenever the terrible-tempered old woman is restless," Marusia's mother had warned, "her hut roams through the woods on chicken legs, so that Baba Yaga may search for bad Russian children to cook in a stew."

Marusia forgot the wild turnips. She began to run, first one way and then another.

Marusia stopped running! She stood very still.

Ahead of her, in a clearing, stood Baba Yaga's hut. The hut was surrounded by a fence of bones and skulls.

Marusia hid behind a tree. She could hear noises inside the hut, as though someone were opening and shutting doors and rattling jars. The hut became silent and Baba Yaga leaned out of the door. Her wild hair waved about her face. Her nose, that looked like a rainspout, quivered and sniffed at the clearing. She clawed at the air with her long bony fingers, gnashed her iron teeth and snarled, "I think I smell a bad Russian child."

Then Baba Yaga disappeared into her dark hut. Marusia was too frightened to move and she felt strangely tired. She leaned against the trunk of the tree and fell asleep.

When Marusia awoke she was sitting in a large pan, surrounded by potatoes and onions.

A lean cat was lying beside the stove dreaming of fish heads and rats.

And Baba Yaga was bent over a table. She was pulling petals from flowers and making neat piles of stems and leaves. Her elbows flapped beneath her cloak like vulture's wings.

Baba Yaga whirled from the table and her cat screeched into the air. The old woman shook salt and pepper into the pan.

"Pardon me, Baba Yaga, but I am a good Russian girl," said Marusia in a very uncertain voice (she was thinking of her family without turnips for their supper).

"A *good* Russian girl!" Baba Yaga shuddered as though Marusia were a toadstool. "I can't eat a good Russian girl for my dinner!" The old woman pulled Marusia out of the pan.

"But I can make you cook my dinner — and sweep the hut — and clean the clearing."

So Marusia swept and cleaned the rest of the day. Then she cooked Baba Yaga's dinner. She lit a fire under the samovar to heat water for Baba Yaga's tea. The old woman ate a meal large enough for ten men. Her stomach rumbled. She offered nothing to Marusia or to the cat.

Baba Yaga's hut was a quiet place, except for the old hag's grumbling. Her cat never purred and birds never chirped or dared to fly near the hut. So Marusia was startled when she heard a noise outside.

In the last light of day Marusia saw a horseman, dressed all in black, ride a black horse past the hut. He vanished into the gloom of night.

Marusia looked to see if Baba Yaga had noticed the horseman, but Baba Yaga had climbed up onto the stove. The old woman yawned and shifted from one warm place to another until she was settled and snoring. Her cat licked the supper dishes until they were clean, then he fell asleep. Marusia fell asleep, too tired to be hungry.

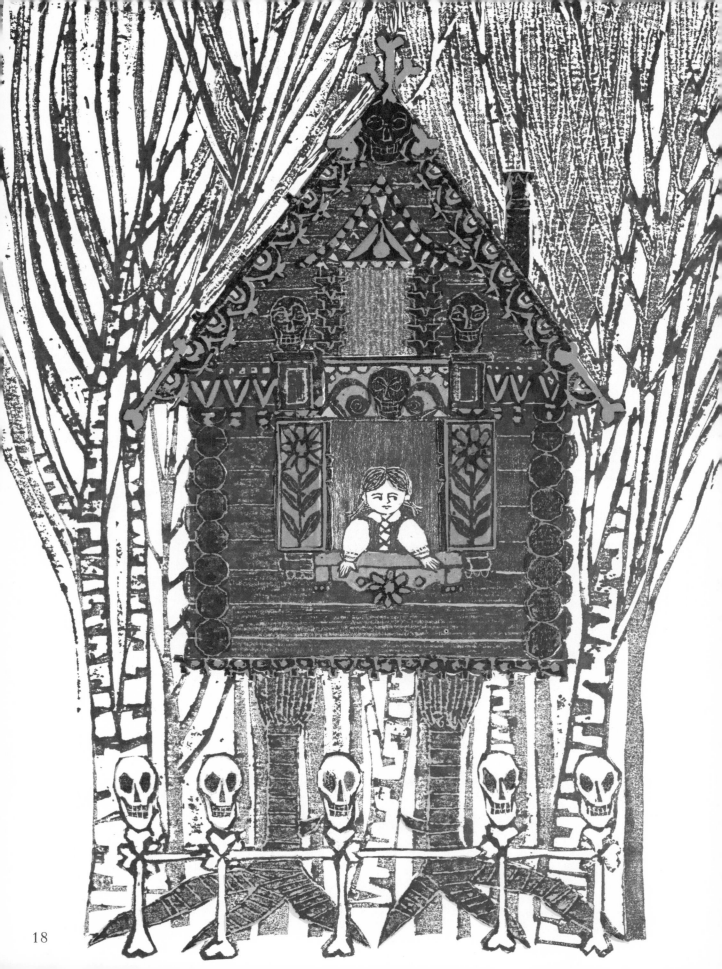

Marusia was awakened by another mysterious horseman. He was dressed all in white and rode a white horse from out of the forest. He galloped across the clearing, and up into the sky. It was a new day.

Baba Yaga was not in the hut but the cat was coiled by the door.

Suddenly, the rising sun disappeared behind swirling black clouds. The sky rumbled with thunder and cracked with lightning. Tree boughs snapped, blew across the clearing, and scratched against the hut.

Baba Yaga swooped out of the storm riding in a mortar. She was steering the mortar with a pestle and sweeping away her traces with a birch twig broom. Baba Yaga jumped to the clearing and the mortar and pestle vanished into the air.

Baba Yaga's cape smelled of smoke and sailed wildly about her. Toads, black beetles and mice darted from under her feet. Bats and owls flew from her hair.

Baba Yaga tickled one of the chicken legs underneath her hut and chanted, "Izbushka, Izbushka, lower your door to me." The chicken legs of the hut, called Izbushka, bent to the ground and Baba Yaga climbed inside.

Baba Yaga emptied a bag of leaves and flowers onto the table. Then she turned to Marusia and hissed, "You say nothing!"

"I don't dare," said Marusia timidly, "but I would like to ask . . ."

"Ask!" interrupted Baba Yaga. "But remember, every question that you ask will make me one year older."

"I only wish to ask," whispered Marusia, "about what I have seen. Last evening a horseman, dressed all in black, rode a black horse through the clearing. Who was he?"

"He was my moonless night," answered Baba Yaga. "He is my obedient servant."

"Early this morning I was awakened by another horseman, dressed in white. He rode a white horse into the sky. Who was he?"

"My fair day," the old woman said with great pride. Then she turned and shuffled across the creaking floor on squeaky shoes.

Baba Yaga stopped in front of a cabinet. She turned a key between a pair of teeth that grinned from the cabinet doors. The teeth snapped a few times, then the doors parted. Inside the cabinet, almost one hundred jars were covered with spiders and webs and filled with leaves, herbs, roots, stems and withered berries.

Baba Yaga could sip boiled berries and crushed autumn leaves and stretch to five times her size. She would sprawl from one corner of the hut to the other until her hair tumbled from the window, her feet dangled from the doorway, and her nose sniffed up the chimney.

Baba Yaga could brew a few thorns and cherry pits with birch sap and then shrink to a tiny size — small enough to hide inside a thimble.

Baba Yaga searched day after day for rare herbs or hidden seeds to put in her cabinet. But there was just one jar in the cabinet that she could not fill.

"One more jar," Marusia heard Baba Yaga mumble. "It waits for the petals of the sunflower that is black. If I can find the black sunflower I will be able to live another two hundred years. I will be able to cure any spell."

She turned to Marusia. "You're too quiet, little girl!"

"I have only another question to ask," whispered Marusia.

"One more question is all you may have, or I will grow too old. Choose it wisely!" Baba Yaga locked her cabinet; the teeth clamped shut.

"Baba Yaga, I wonder if I might have some turnips?"

"Turnips? When I have sausage and cabbage and plump fruit pies?"

"I was sent to the village to buy turnips," continued Marusia, "but I lost the money my mother gave me, and . . ."

"Then you *are* a bad Russian girl!"

Baba Yaga put Marusia back in the pan. Then she jumped out of the hut to gather mushrooms and parsley for the stew.

Baba Yaga kicked a rooster out of her parsley patch and picked some parsley.

She found a hedgehog sitting on top of a big mushroom eating
a mushroom. The hedgehog looked up at Baba Yaga and said,
"Please, Babushka, don't kick me, for I have suffered enough."

Baba Yaga thought the hedgehog might make a nice goulash. "That should ease his suffering!" she said to herself and she put the hedgehog into the pan with Marusia. She sprinkled them both with parsley and mushrooms.

"How do you do," said the hedgehog to Marusia.

"Wherever did you learn to speak so well?" said Marusia.

The hedgehog told Marusia his story.

THE HEDGEHOG'S STORY

"Far, far away from here a tsar and a tsarina live in a beautiful palace. They have over one hundred million rubles, but they have no children.

"Many years ago a strange flower bloomed in the palace garden. The tsarina would often sit in her garden and admire the flower. One day she thought aloud; If only I could have a son, were he no bigger than a hedgehog.

"The marvelous flower was enchanted. A hedgehog was born to the tsar and the tsarina."

The hedgehog sighed and then continued, "The tsar and the tsarina had me educated by tutors, and by the time I was seven I had learned all that I could.

"When the country learned that the tsar and the tsarina had a hedgehog instead of a son, the people laughed and laughed, louder and louder, until the tsar and the tsarina could hear the laughter over the palace wall. The tsar and the tsarina were ashamed."

The hedgehog leaned back against an onion. His voice trembled. "They set me upon a rooster and banished me to the forest, hoping that I would be eaten by a wolf or a bear.

"That was over a year ago; since then I have hardly had enough to eat. I know only the ways of an educated person and life as a hedgehog bewilders me."

Marusia felt sorry for the little hedgehog. She thought awhile, then she said, "The flower that you speak of, it must be very unusual."

The hedgehog drew close to Marusia. "It is a most curious flower. It is a sunflower, but it is black."

Marusia stood up in the pan. "Baba Yaga has searched all Russia for the black sunflower! Tell me, little hedgehog, where is the palace that you have talked about?"

"Only I know the way," answered the hedgehog.

"Quiet!" growled Baba Yaga. She clapped a cover over the pan.

Marusia and the hedgehog whispered for awhile inside the pan. Then they lifted the cover — just high enough for Marusia to shout, "I know where the black sunflower is!"

Then they slammed the cover down and waited.

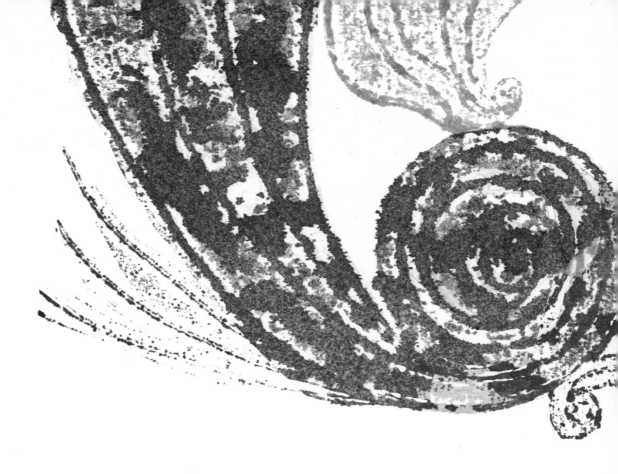

Baba Yaga pulled the cover away from the pan. Her eyes were as wide as two moons. Her iron teeth chattered.

"What did you say about the black sunflower?"

"If you will give me some turnips I will tell you," offered Marusia.

"When the sunflower is mine the turnips will be yours," bargained Baba Yaga. "Where may the black sunflower be found?"

"If we follow the hedgehog he will lead us to it," said Marusia. She helped the hedgehog out of the pan.

Baba Yaga and Marusia flew above the hedgehog for three nights and four days until they reached a mountain.

The hedgehog climbed halfway up the mountain and disappeared into a hole. Baba Yaga had to shrink herself to half her size and squeeze Marusia into the hole behind her. They followed the hedgehog through a long winding tunnel until they reached daylight once again.

A magnificent palace sparkled in front of them. The mortar and pestle reappeared, and they all flew over the palace wall and into the garden.

39

Baba Yaga leaped from the mortar and trampled over lilies, lilacs and roses until she had found the black sunflower. She pulled at the enchanted flower, and as soon as the black sunflower left the earth the hedgehog turned into a little boy named Dmitri.

Baba Yaga was in too much of a hurry to notice that the hedge-hog had turned into a little boy. She flew off in a swirling black cloud, with the black sunflower and the children; and they were gone before the tsar and the tsarina knew anyone had been in the palace garden.

After they had returned to the hut, and Marusia had reminded her, Baba Yaga gave Marusia some turnips . . . then Baba Yaga put Marusia and Dmitri back in the pan.

"This is a fine reward," cried Marusia, "after we helped you find the black sunflower."

"You have your turnips — that is enough reward!" snapped Baba Yaga, "and naughty girls make such a tasty stew."

"But I am not a naughty girl!" said Marusia.

"You lost your mother's money; that is very naughty!" said Baba Yaga. She rubbed garlic around the pan.

"But I did get what I was sent for." Marusia sneezed. The garlic was very strong. "Turnips!"

Baba Yaga lifted the good girl out of the pan. "So you did," she sighed. "But the hedgehog will be good for the stew!"

"But I am not a hedgehog!" laughed Dmitri, although he was still wearing a hedgehog suit.

Baba Yaga studied the little boy. "These eyes of fire do not see too well," she said. "Why, you are a *little boy*. You would make a terrible hedgehog stew!"

The happy children ran around the hut. They poked into cupboards and took books from the shelves. They chased the cat and begged Baba Yaga to open her cabinet.

Baba Yaga, who had been used to a quiet life, with only her cat and treasures, grumbled, "I can't have children around here. Their endless questions make my old bones ache."

Early the next morning, when the horseman rode his white horse out of the night, Baba Yaga took the children and ran out to the clearing. She stopped the rider and lifted the children onto his horse. Then Baba Yaga ran back to her hut. The chicken legs bent to the ground and the old woman climbed inside and slammed the door.

Marusia and Dmitri rode off into the dawn. They rode out of the clearing, beyond the forest, and away from Baba Yaga. They rode all the way back to Marusia's cottage.

And they had turnips for supper.